A NEW YEAR'S TALE

by *Vladimir Dudintsev*

NOT BY BREAD ALONE

A NEW YEAR'S TALE

by

VLADIMIR DUDINTSEV

A Dutton **dep** *Paperback*

Everyman

Translated by
GABRIELLA AZRAEL
Illustrations by JIM MCMULLAN

New York
E. P. DUTTON & CO., INC.
1960

A NEW YEAR'S TALE

A NEW YEAR'S TALE

I LIVE IN A fairy-tale world, in a fairy-tale country, in a city created by my imagination. Wonderful adventures happen to people there, and I've had my share of adventures. I'm going to tell you something about them because at New Year's time a man is in the mood to listen to stories of make-believe. We will be talking about the tricks that time plays upon us. But time is immense, and is everywhere. In a fairy-tale world, time is just as reliable as is standard time in Moscow. So I take this risk in beginning my story: maybe some curious person will get so interested in my imaginary country that he'll think I'm describing an actual, nonimaginary life.

A mysterious bird flew into our town—an owl. It made several men very happy with its visits. The first man was my immediate boss, the head of the laboratory for Sun Research where I work. The second man was the neurophysician, my old friend from school. The owl chose me for the third visit. That bird was—remarkable. It would not have been a bad idea if people had studied its habits and had made a drawing of it for the bird books.

At this time I had already published scientific papers on some peculiar features of sunlight. I had received a scholarly degree, had become a consultant to several commissions and was hastening to climb higher. Imitating my venerable elders, I had learned to hold my head as they did, to think over questions unhurriedly as they did, to raise my eyebrows as they did, and to deliver my valued, considered judgment in a singsong voice. Still another feature: I had grown used to taking care of my expensive overcoat. In our office there are cupboards and, mimicking the elders, I hung in my closet a wooden coat hanger engraved with my initials.

Being a man possessed of certain modest talents, I, on the advice of one academician, had trained myself to jot down thoughts that occurred to me unexpectedly. It is known that the most valuable thoughts are not those which we struggle over for hours at the desk but those which spring up like the wind—most often when one is walking down the street. I jotted down these thoughts and forgot about them. But our janitress knew well that in the drawers of my desk magical pieces of paper were collecting that would burn like gunpowder. She got into the habit of cleaning my desk and fed the furnaces of our office with them.

But beneath the shell of solidity there was a child within me (by the way, this was true also of my boss—a Doctor of Science). This child with puffed-out cheeks sometimes came to the surface, especially in those evening hours when we bachelors sat in our apartment stupefied like drunkards in front of the television and for hours followed the flashing legs of the football players on the pale blue screen.

As you see, I am here sparing myself least of all. I am

presenting many aspects of my character and with full awareness will present still more for your judgment, and will myself be the first judge. A short time ago my eyes seem to have opened; precisely from the day when the owl paid me its first visit. I have it to thank for opening my eyes.

For example, I saw my dispute with S., a corresponding member of a provincial Academy of Sciences, in a new light. Five years ago he called a well-known article of mine "the fruit of idle speculations." I had to respond. In a new article I, as it were in passing, refuted S.'s basic theses. In my opinion, I hit the mark with such words as "It is precisely this that Candidate of Sciences S. is trying to prove." (I knew well that although he is a corresponding member of the Academy, he is only a candidate just as I am.) S. answered my attack with a brochure in which, incidentally, as it were, he said that I fixed the results of my experiments to fit a theory, putting "theory" in quotation marks. Soon afterward I printed a long article on my new observations of the sun that confirmed the "theory" in quotes and blasted S.'s calculations to smithereens. "The battleship took a torpedo amidships," as my comrades said on this occasion. I didn't mention S.'s name in my article. I knew that my enemy wouldn't endure this second torpedo. I simply said "some authors." But the battleship rose up and answered.

And so forth. This war that dragged on for five years wore my nerves raw—and not only mine.

But more to the point. One morning we all gathered in our laboratory, hung our overcoats on the hangers, and before going to work on our researches we called a meeting together as usual. Our senior and respected boss, a Doctor of Science, began the discussion. In his free time he had a strange hobby: he collected stone axes, ancient coins, and books. I think that the chief meaning of his peaceful life lay in this hobby and not in our work.

"A curious thing," he said, inviting us to listen. "Not long ago, while trying to figure out an inscription on a stone slab, I found this image."

And he showed us a sheet of white paper on which was drawn in India ink a large-eared owl.

"I managed to read the inscription," the boss said proudly. "There was some sort of name and then: 'And his life was nine hundred years.' "

"Y-yes," dreamily said one of my colleagues in the group, a dandy and a practical joker. "Even four hundred would be enough for me."

"Nonsense!" interrupted a broad-shouldered, dry, aged man who was usually silent. He was sitting next to me and was distinguished from all of us by his conscious indifference to clothes, by his taciturnity, and by his unique capacity for work. "What do you need four hundred years for?" he said. "You aren't in a hurry anyway."

"I want to direct your attention"—the boss raised his voice, letting us know that we had interrupted him in the middle—"I'd like your attention! Such words have been found in many countries at various times. In one desert there stands a gigantic owl of granite. In our locality mine is the first such find. I am entitled to boast." Here the boss broke into a smile. "This owl and this inscription are my personal discovery. I dug up this stone in my own garden."

We congratulated him on his luck, looked once more at the owl, and went to our own places.

"I will certainly manage to discover the meaning of this drawing," said the boss. "Afterward I will write an article."

"Perhaps these hieroglyphics indicate a man who knew how to dispose of his time in the best possible way," I suggested.

"Possibly. But that still has to be confirmed."

"But nine hundred years of life!" I couldn't refrain from this exclamation. Was such a long life really possible?

"Everything is possible," my broad-shouldered neighbor, who was always busy, barked without ceasing work.

"What do you mean by that?" politely inquired the boss.

"Time is a riddle," was the answer, still more cryptic.

"Yes, time is a riddle." The boss picked up this interesting thought. He took down from the wall an hourglass, turned it over, and placed it before him on the desk.

"It is flowing," he said, staring at the sand. "And look at what happens: the instant we live can be compared with the tiniest grain of sand, with an infinitely small granule. It is disappearing right now."

And suddenly I felt a pain somewhere in my chest. I had had in my life several months of unexpected, unique love; and those months, now that I looked back on them in pain, merged into a single instant, became a grain of sand draining to the bottom of the hourglass. And there was now nothing left. As if nothing had been. I sighed. If one could turn back the clock!

"Excuse me, boss," the director of our personnel department interrupted. "What is the result of your theory, if I may call it that? If time is but a point, does that mean that we don't have our heroic past? Don't we have our future place in the sun?"

He loved to ask direct questions loudly, as if he had caught a man in a horrible crime.

"I beg your pardon if I said something wrong," answered our peace-loving boss. "But I don't think I've had time to formulate any sort of theory. This is all a joke, a fantasy."

"A strange sort of fancy. All the same, there are limits."

"Friend!" suddenly shouted our disheveled, eternally busy eccentric. We all turned around. "The new that we seek is almost always found beyond the limits."

And, opening his mouth—he had this mannerism—he silently began to laugh in the personnel director's stern face. We saw a new side of our comrade's character.

Two years we had sat in the same room with him but didn't know the man. We saw only that he shaved rarely and threw his overcoat on a chair. We noticed that half of the buttons on the overcoat were missing. And finally, we saw that our colleague did the work of four. But we hadn't really managed to get to know him.

"You know, I will now tell you an interesting story." Again we heard the voice of this comrade who was eternally bent over his work.

All of us were surprised: the man for the first time had decided to loosen up, to waste his time in conversation with us. I hadn't thought that the conversation about longevity would so relax him.

"Only now I must run to the basement and lay out some equipment so that time will not be lost," he said, and quickly went out.

"Is he a queer one or not?" someone asked.

"I don't think so," retorted the practical joker. "A lady comes to see him sometimes. I live next door to him. A young lady. I bumped into her once on the stairway. She didn't notice a thing. Blind with love."

"You know he has a unique antique watch. It runs

with unusual precision and has to be set only once a year." The boss said this.

"And so, my friend!" Our tousled, graying comrade (whom we had just gotten to know that morning), our industrious colleague, came in again, sat down at his place, and took up his slide rule. "You say nine hundred years. But do you know that time can stand still or it can fly swiftly? Haven't you ever waited for someone?"

"Yes, time can pass very slowly," said the boss.

"It can stand still! You remember the story about the scholars who raised lotus blossoms from seeds that had lain in a stone coffin for two thousand years? For those lotus blossoms, time stood still. I tell you, time can hang back or jump forward!"

As he said this, he adjusted his slide rule and wrote something down. He was able to continue working during the conversation.

"I'll tell you a story now which, despite its moral, will interest you." And as he began, it seemed to me that he turned in my direction as if his words were meant exclusively for me.

"Several years ago, in a certain kingdom, in a certain state, and, to be precise, in our city, this took place: one Sunday in the Park of Culture, in one of the darkest corners, a group of sixty, or maybe a hundred, well-dressed men gathered for a discussion they had decided to hold outside. Later it became known that in our park,

a symposium, so to say, of bandits and thieves had met, to form a 'Brotherhood,' as they say. They had, in this gang, severe rules, and a death penalty for breaking them. Those who were accepted into the 'law' had to be sponsored. A new member of the society had a motto tattooed on his chest—several words to show straight off that he was in."

"What relation does this story have to our discussion of time?" the boss asked gently. "Or haven't you finished yet, perhaps?"

"Yes, I'm not through yet. The relation is very direct. I'm just now coming to the subject. The meeting of the Brotherhood resulted in six death sentences, five of which were carried out. They couldn't catch the sixth one because this was a complicated business. I'll say right off who he was and what his crime was. He was the head, the president—'pakhan' (in the group's word)—of the Brotherhood, the oldest and cleverest of the bandits. He was locked up in some distant prison, and in his solitude the idea must have come to him that he had never done anything essential in life, or gotten anything from it, and that he had little time left. He figured it out this way: the whole meaning of a bandit's life is to lift other people's riches, gold and precious things. But the value and authority of things in human society were falling catastrophically."

"Seems as if he was quite a theoretician, your bandit," the personnel director commented ironically.

"Yes, he was a serious person," our eccentric agreed. I felt sorry for him. "This criminal who was responsible for a lot of misery had begun to read books of late. Books—a terrific source of strength! He read many books. He was in no hurry to leave prison—he was satisfied just to read and think in his stone cell, and his 'legal' comrades could get any book at all for their leader, even if it was kept in the cellar of the State Treasury behind seven seals. Yes—and so he saw that the authority of precious things was falling catastrophically. Sometime long ago, rich people, princes, built pools in ocean harbors to breed sharks. They fed the sharks on human flesh —they threw slaves in to them. To put such a shark on a holiday table was considered extremely chic. But now we can't even consider the amusements of our ancestors without shuddering. Gold at one time was an anonymous metal dozing peacefully underground. Then man gave it a name and value. It was considered extremely chic to sport gold on one's clothes or weapons. Now no one would allow himself to appear in public with a gold chain across his stomach or even a gold tiepin. The authority of gold is falling. Where is the prestige of precious cloth? I assure you that today the most valuable cloth is going out of fashion. To walk materialistic paths today is a sign of spiritual backwardness."

"Look, if you please, how this bandit straightened out his materialistic values! Tell me what takes the place of things?" asked the personnel director. This story bothered him a little because, as it happened, he was wearing an expensive suit with broad shoulders, and his wife, who had somehow gotten into the laboratory, was carrying on her arm a heavy silver fox coat.

"What things are we talking about? There are things and things, the bandit observed, and fell to thinking. He understood that the value of things was being supplanted inevitably by the beauty of the human soul, which can't be bought or stolen. You can't make anyone love you at gunpoint. The soul's beauty is free. It has come into first place, while gold and velvet have taken a lesser position. Now Cinderellas in cotton dresses triumph over princesses dressed in silk, because the value of a cheap dress lies in its cut, and that value is immaterial. A dress sketch represents the taste and character of the person who chose the sketch. It was no accident that many princesses who still had souls began to dress like Cinderellas. And if we meet one all decked out in furs and precious cloth, we don't wonder over the richness of her clothing but try to avoid such a spiritual monster who advertises herself as such.

"My bandit suddenly saw that in all his life he had never had such things as human approval, friendship, true love, and had tried all his life not to value them. Something like a monetary reform took place. Yes . . ." The storyteller's voice was hoarse. He coughed. "But the people, love, and friendship he needed existed on earth.

He knew them—there was a woman. But he couldn't even see her. He didn't dare risk showing himself.

"So this man wrote all his thoughts down in a long letter to the Brotherhood and announced that he was 'defrocking,' going into the society of normal working people, and he intended somehow to fight for what he'd never known in life but which was suddenly, as they say, his whole existence. The prison administration printed this letter of his in a special pamphlet. You understand, the document was very powerful and it was necessary to make use of it.

"So, look at the position our 'pakhan' was in. During his life he had been sentenced to more than two hundred years in prison, none of which he had served. He understood that the government wouldn't change this number of years. On the other hand, he knew better than anyone the laws of the Brotherhood and was aware that his comrades would not forgive his defection and a knife was waiting for him somewhere. But he had to live at least a few more years to accomplish the things for which he had taken this step. He fled from the fate his comrades had devised for him. He was rich enough, and as can happen in fairy tales, doctors were found who knew how to graft the skin on his face and head and to change his hair. They did something to his voice. They were great artists.

"The bandit received clean documents and became a new man. In three years he graduated from two institutes. Now he is winding up his affairs—his great dream of giving something to the people."

"Well, fine." I interrupted him because he was constantly looking at me. "What has this to do with our discussion? Has it to do with the fact that time can stand or fly, or with what is written on the stone: 'And his life was nine hundred years'?"

"There is a direct connection. The executors of the sentence are hunting this man. They are steadily stalking his tracks. They will certainly overtake him. The man has very little time left. Time—do you understand? And the man intended to live his life over again for two or three years. What would have happened if he had lived all his years thus? His life would perhaps have been equal to more than nine hundred years."

"You have in mind, of course, the content of life and not its length?" said the boss.

"It is certainly clear that you don't save much time!" My neighbor was angry. "Yes, yes, yes! The content. That with which we fill the vessel of life. We must fill it up with only the very strongest delights, with sensations of the greatest joy."

"Well, it is already clear." Again the voice of the personnel director was heard. "This is preaching of the purest egoism. You would like to delight in everything. But I think that it is necessary to work for the people. Well, what do you think?"

"You are backward; that's what I think. You have to

be led by the hand. You suppose that joy and sensation are sins to which you secretly give yourself up within the privacy of your own four walls. But work for the people is a public obligation. My bandit is progressive in comparison with you. He has tried all your joys and he is fed up with them. He now recognizes only a single joy, that which you consider a stern obligation."

"Tell us," said the boss after a minute's silence, "how do you know such details? After all, the man has changed his face, his name . . . probably he is not such a fool as to reveal himself to the first person he meets."

"I am not the first person he has met."

"You ought to give him up to the authorities if you are a conscientious person," the personnel director suddenly observed. "He committed so many crimes and broke from prison."

"Not for anything," said our comrade. "Not for anything. He is no longer a bandit. He's not dangerous now. He is even useful. When he has accomplished his goal, he will give himself up to the people."

Then he took out of his pocket his renowned watch, a heavy globe on a steel chain.

"Excuse me. I should go look at the indicators on my instruments." And he got up. At the door he paused.

"All should contemplate this story. And you especially." And he looked point-blank at me. "I think it possible that you will consider the experience of these people and stop playing games—that you will put a period to your fruitless polemic with that corresponding member of the Academy."

How could I then have supposed that life would involve even me in this story, make me its second hero? His double!

In order to confirm a suspicion that suddenly sprang up in me, I went down into the cellar after a half hour. The door creaked slightly, the door behind which this man sat surrounded by sparkling glass and copper instruments. The sound was barely audible, but he jumpèd aside so abruptly that he shattered several phials.

"Excuse me," I said.

"You are confirming your suspicion?" he asked, growing calmer.

"You aren't careful," I answered.

"I'm not afraid of you." He turned back to his instruments.

Now when I had definitely established what I had earlier only suspected, I understood several other things. (I will keep silent about them until it is time.)

Not long before these occurrences, I had, incomprehensibly, become the object of someone's interest. Some sort of shadow followed me tirelessly through the streets of the city, followed me from afar. I didn't manage to get a glimpse of the face of my pursuer, although he was in no hurry to hide. For his observation point he (or she) chose dark archways or entranceways. He would come out directly into the sun, but as soon as I reached into my pocket for my glasses, my friend took off into an archway. Several times I approached those gates or entrances where this person was hiding who was so fascinated by me, but found no one. Not so long ago the first light and pure snow fell. I was going along an empty street late in the evening when I heard steps behind me, and before I had time to turn around, I realized that it was he (or she). I turned and saw something like a cloak or dress-suit tails swirling around the corner. I dashed in pursuit like a madman, but when I swung around the corner I saw a completely empty white lane. I examined the snow and found no traces. True, I remember that several cross-shaped imprints like the tracks of a huge chicken foot were melting into the light, airy snow.

In the cellar I whispered all this to my comrade. He shook my hand and answered, "Thank you. I myself have noticed something. And now go. I must hurry. As you see, time is rushing me. And it wouldn't hurt you to speed your tempo. Who knows what can happen . . ."

We were both working on the same problem but were using different approaches. One of us was right, one wrong. But it was worth it to make mistakes that could show the right approach. We were looking for a way to condense sunlight. The product we hoped to get was going to guarantee months and years of sunlight and warmth to that faraway continent whose inhabitants did not know what sun was. On our planet, you see, one side is never lighted by the sun. There, there is only night and winter. That my colleague was grappling with this problem was proof of something for me: before me stood this extraordinary bandit chief, seeking life. Would he be able to fulfill his plan in a year, even two years?

You see, I'm a man who values things highly, and I mark time for a year or two wondering where to start, because to start a research project means burying oneself for ten good years. What if the whole laboratory had worked on the project! But, thank God, we were the only ones allowed to work on it. There were many against us in this project. Almost all the members of the Academic Council considered us dreamers.

But it turned out that there were not two years but only a few hours left to this man. The next morning they telephoned me from the hospital. They had found my extraordinary bandit the night before, covered with blood, near our entrance (we lived in the same building). He had several deep knife wounds in his back. The whole institute was thrown into an uproar and began to call for the most renowned doctors. It was no use. At noon the institute officials telephoned the office of the burial organization.

His death, which he himself had, as it were, predicted, affected us strongly. For several days all of us, on meeting together in the morning at work, exchanged sympathetic glances. I proved a coward. First I gave way to panic and even grew thinner. I was unable to listen to any extraneous discussions not precisely to the point and worked intensely for a week. But after a week, when I received the new issue of our scientific journal and read in the table of contents the name of Corresponding Member of the Academy S., I then and there flew into a rage and forgot about everything on earth except that piece of paper covered with printed symbols. Nervously, I leafed through the journal and at once caught sight of a footnote set in small type. (The most caustic expressions are always set in small type.) There, surrounded by politely venomous words, I saw my name. And my life turned back into the old channel. Paper, paper—who invented you? I dropped work and, urged on by all my rooters, wrote an article, including not just one but three footnotes. They should have completely annihilated my enemy. The whole department composed those footnotes. And if you should want to see us at this work, I can help you: go into the Tretyakov Gallery and look at Repin's picture "The Zaporozhians Writing to the Sultan of Turkey." In this picture our entire department is depicted—with our boss heehawing and holding his stomach and me sitting at the desk, wearing glasses, with pen in hand.

Falling into the old familiar rut, I quite forgot about the object that was following me, from around corners, from archways and entranceways. After the first distressing days which, as you know, follow funerals, the dress-

suit tail did not appear. I was sure then that one of the
bandits who had carried out the sentence on the dead
man had been following me.

But soon after I received the newspaper with my article
in answer to my primordial enemy S., more exactly on
the very day when I came out of the editorial office
where they had ordered still another article from me, I
felt up and down my spine that someone was looking at
me. I looked around and saw no one. No, but looking
carefully I nonetheless caught sight of some sort of figure
in a dark gap in the second floor of a half-ruined house
that workers were demolishing. It at once stepped aside,
behind a wall.

This was, as it happened, the day on which I was to
mark my thirtieth birthday. I wanted to invite my comrades to celebrate. But as you can see, while it was still
afternoon, the first shadow was cast over my holiday.

I went home and climbed up to my floor. In the hall
where we all watched television in the evenings a comrade awaited me—the dandy and practical joker.

"Well, shall we celebrate today?"

"I'm not quite well," I answered. "We'll have to postpone it."

"It's not good to be sulky on such a noteworthy day.
Thirty years—man's best age."

And right there he gave me a gift of a bright-colored
necktie.

"Well, shall we celebrate? I'll knock you off your

feet," he whispered. "I was lucky enough to get some really rare wine."

By the way, while talking with him I noticed in the farthest corner a woman whom I didn't know. I sensed somehow that she must have been waiting for me a long time. Then she rose and took a step toward me, and from then on I heard nothing that my comrade was saying to me. The woman was about thirty, with sloping shoulders, and very pretty. Her beauty was in the special, sweet imperfections of her face and figure and especially in her direct, melancholy gaze. This beauty was suddenly reflected and heightened in the woman's quiet, low voice. I at once remembered that other golden speck of dust which long ago flowed down into its place in the hourglass. That one lay forgotten, inanimate, nonexistent, but this one moved toward me.

"They asked me to give you this for your birthday," she said in an almost official tone, and presented me the familiar antique watch, big and heavy on its steel chain. "And this too." She took an envelope out of her handbag and gave it to me.

I asked, "Is it from him?"

"Yes," answered the woman.

I wondered if the dead man had known real love—love that cannot be bought or stolen. But she guessed what I was thinking and stopped me by raising her finger.

"There was love," she whispered. "And is. And will be. But he was not sure of me. I teased him. Do you know what I mean? . . . And when they admitted me to the hospital, I shouted at him for a whole hour: 'Yes, yes, yes!' But he didn't hear."

I lowered my head. My poor comrade. I know what it is like.

Putting the watch in my pocket, I accompanied the woman downstairs and then returned.

"That's the same one," said our dandy softly. "She used to go see the bandit and didn't notice anyone. She was blind from love."

And he laughingly added:

"She noticed you, though. Watch out!"

I went into my own room and ripped open the envelope.

"They will give you this envelope if I am murdered," my dead friend had written. "You are a talented person. I am writing to you precisely because you know more about me than the others and perhaps value time more than the others. Life is given once and it is necessary to drink it in huge swallows. One must seize what is most precious. And what is most precious I have already told you. Not gold or rags. I want you to find a great joy in life. You should remember the dark continent where millions of people are now living. Let the day on which you receive this letter be the day of your real birth . . ."

I stopped reading for a moment, for a strong, happy thought that suddenly sprang up interrupted me. "I am happier than he." That is what came into my head. "I still have half my life ahead of me, or two-thirds. I don't have to hurry. I'll have time for everything."

A dark, heavy mass covered my window. It was probably because some workman was on a ladder there. Turning the page to continue the letter, I went toward the window to be nearer the light. But, I thought, what would a workman be doing there in the winter? I looked up and shuddered: on the other side of the wall, on a railing under the window, a huge owl with shaggy ears and gray side whiskers was sitting and—this was the strangest thing—looking distorted as if it had been drawn by a primitive artist. It was my owl. It was the first time I had seen it. I waved the letter at it—"Shoo!" This made no impression on the owl whatsoever. This sudden mystery shocked me and I even began to sweat a little out of fear. "Whew!" I took a breath with difficulty and wiped my brow. The owl just sat straight and still, as all owls do. I took another breath, wiped my brow, and carefully left the room. I don't remember how I got out onto the street into the cold. Where should I go? To where my friend from school, the experienced neurophysician, was working? My case would interest him, and he would take care of me.

Walking rapidly along the purplish boulevard as the shadows darkened toward evening, I heard behind me a

strange jumping step. I looked back. Someone was standing behind the nearest tree. I distinctly made out a shaggy ear and protruding wing. That owl was as big as I was!

The doctor was busy. I waited for a long time outside the white doors of his office, listening to the regular, hurrying footsteps. Finally, the doors opened and my friend appeared in a white gown and cap pulled down to his eyebrows. He was emaciated and pale from work and lack of sleep.

"Well, what's new?" someone somewhere cried out.

"Nothing." He was twitching nervously as he looked at me and saw nothing.

I got up. The doctor recovered slowly. He recognized me and took my hand. "If you've come on a social visit, this is not the time."

"This isn't a social visit."

"Well then, come." He took my hand and looked at the tips of my fingers. "How old are you?"

"Thirty."

"I forgot that we're the same age. What's your trouble? Is someone following you?" he asked.

"Yes, if you only knew what it is! So awfully strange. You'll laugh at me."

"Do you want me to show you? Come with me." He took me into his office and looked toward the window.

"My owl!" I whispered.

"Not just yours, mine too. Give me your hands; let

me see. Yes, yes." He went to his table and turned away. Then he turned back to me. "You'll find out sooner or later. So make it sooner. You have only one year left to live."

The floor collapsed under me and I would have fallen if my friend hadn't gotten me into a chair.

I know that there are people who aren't afraid of death: these brave souls need no protection. But I admit it to you—I was trembling with fear. After I finish my work I can die, but not now!

"I don't believe it," I whispered.

"You'd better stand up and leave," the doctor said, raising his eyebrows, obviously getting nervous. "You have a whole year of life."

"I don't believe it."

"Get out of here!" he shouted suddenly. "You're wasting my time! I'm sick myself. I have only a year and a half myself!"

But at the door he stopped me and said quickly, almost in a patter, "It's an ancient disease, and, in general, talented people suffer from an especially virulent form. Passive people get quietly sick and die unnoticed."

"And you haven't discovered anything?"

"We've discovered a great deal. But we can't cure. We do know this much . . ."

And he said this inexplicable thing: "He who sees the owl distinctly is half saved."

And he closed the door behind me.

"Did I see it distinctly? I'll have to see," I thought.

And suddenly I heard something ticking in the silence: the watch, the bandit's gift, was doing its work, counting off the seconds. Listening to their noisy progress, I got out the heavy watch and the carved key. Twenty times I turned the key and finally felt it stop—there! The watch was wound for a year.

"I must hurry! Think of everything," I said to myself. For the first time in my life I hurried in the real sense. That is, I was composed.

The clean, cool evening met me with cheerful lights and the noise of automobiles and the distant twinkling of stars.

"I'll think about and look at the stars," I decided. And the starry sky lowered itself so that I could see its mighty endlessness better.

"All right, then. Flesh dies. Let it die. But thought, thought! Really, will it disappear?" I closed my eyes.

"I won't disappear," my thought spoke into the gloom. Unlike feeling, thought was calm. "Look," sounded thought's voice. "The world of civilization lives for several thousand years. But how long do the things men make live? Machines, furniture, clothing—all fall apart in a few decades. So how have we accumulated things? Very simply. We have accumulated thoughts: the secrets of rolling metal, drug formulas, and hardening cement. Burn the books, destroy the secrets of handicraft, and give mankind several decades to forget everything, and man will start out once more on the road up from the Stone Age. And your son—not your grandson—will dig up something you made in your youth, and he'll pray over it like a miracle of God."

From an unseen loud-speaker a waltz floated loudly over the city. I didn't know the composer of the waltz. I didn't even listen to the music. This wasn't an orchestra but horns—not horns but violins—not violins but the voices of my emotions. And when the ancient woodwinds took up the melody, when the woods sang, then it became clear that these were my lost hopes singing in the stuffy box of my short life.

"You want to live," the unknown composer said to me. "Look what those few notes of music that I put down a hundred years ago after my short, unhappy stay among men did to you. Listen; for him who has only a little time, life is brighter and more desirable. It is better not to have and to want than to have and not want! I loved life a great deal and I pass on to you that love."

Then he lowered his voice. "And now listen. In my short life, I knew the greatest happiness. You know what I'm talking about. And you? Has a grateful man squeezed your hand so hard that your heart jumped? Have you looked into eyes filled with tears of love?"

These thoughts stunned me. I'd never had any of this. I had loved but hadn't been loved. I hadn't known great friendship, nor deserved men's gratitude. I lowered my head and no longer listened to the music. The fires faded around me. I heard only one thing—the ticking of the watch. This watch, the bandit's gift, was doing its work, counting off time, my seconds: "Your whole life is ahead of you! A whole year! You were just born! You're younger than you were! Run faster to your work . . . to your friend and love!"

I began to run, and jumped into a taxi. "Faster, faster —to the laboratory!" The driver looked back in amazement at his extraordinary passenger as he shifted into third.

Leaving the car at the entrance, I ran in and up the stairs. In the corridor, near the hotly burning stove, head down, my old janitress was asleep on a chair. I woke her.

"Give me all my papers! The ones I gave you today, this morning. I gave you a whole basketful."

"Oh, dear man!"

I groaned and ran to the incinerator.

"Everything's burned. They burned nicely. Only your papers burn so nicely. You see I got so warm I even fell asleep!"

Tick, tick, tick, the bandit's watch said in my pocket. Biting my lips, I went into my office and began to carry my boxes of instruments out to the street, to the taxi. I had decided to set up a workplace in my home, to work at night. I wanted to be worthy of the deepest gratitude of the people, and I hadn't even begun.

When I appeared on the doorstep of our bachelor apartment carrying my boxes there were several men sitting, as usual, around the television in the living room.

"So, it's been decided that we'll postpone the celebration," the practical joker said to me.

He was turning the knobs of the television set. There on the glass screen the legs of the football players flashed. The fans stood stock-still, their eyes enlarged unnaturally. I heard the ticking of the watch and understood. If our set worked uninterruptedly for two thousand years, these five men would sit there and not move and would be preserved for their descendants like the lotus seeds.

I moved several men and chairs to get them out of the way of my boxes and carried my things into my room and dismissed the cabby.

At home my owl was sitting in its place under the window. Now I viewed it calmly. It was visible in the clear light of the lamp. Did I see it distinctly? I went to the window. We looked at each other for a while. Then it moved along the railing and back, exactly as owls do in the zoo. Bending over, it raised its yellow three-taloned foot, which looked as if it had been dipped in wax, and, as fast as a chicken, combed its beak with its talon. Then it settled down again in a vertical position and fixed on me two cruel circles—its eyes. I saw my owl distinctly!

Then I came to and began to open my boxes and set out my equipment. Within five minutes my room sparkled with glass and copper; it had become a laboratory.

"Will I succeed?" I wondered. "I need at least ten years."

I tried to recall something of the ideas that had been burned up at various times in the laboratory's incinerator. I tried to write them down again, but nothing came.

That would have cut my work in half.

Then I saw the note from the bandit on the floor where I had thrown it earlier. Several lines I had not read at all, and, as it happened, these were the lines which stared up at me from the floor:

"I can be of use to you. Did you understand what was said about the bandit? Then ask the woman standing in front of you, and she'll give you the notebook in which I wrote down all the ideas that you have been burning in the stove for two years. I wanted you to use them, but, you know, you didn't need them then."

"Where can I find her now?" I shouted, dropping the letter. Then I saw the words: "her telephone . . ."

A few seconds later I was standing, as in a fairy tale, among the slow-breathing, wide-eyed men hypnotized by the television set. I put the telephone on one of their shoulders and dialed. Several rings, and then her voice.

From that moment began a new chapter in my new—short—life. It began with a misunderstanding, thanks to my behavior.

"Why didn't you answer?" These words burst from me before I could think how rude they were. "Where is the notebook? Why didn't you give it to me?"

"You didn't ask for it," she answered. "You didn't even read the letter. It said in the note, if you . . ."

"It's obvious that you don't value time!" I burst out. "Forgive me."

And there was silence.

"Why don't you say something?" I shouted again. "The notebook!"

"I'm coming," said the quiet, tender voice.

When I heard her steps I understood suddenly that I was waiting for more than the notebook. From the moment when I saw the woman for the first time, I had been drawn to her as a sliver of wood is drawn to a waterfall. Hadn't the second golden grain of sand dropped into the neck of the hourglass, and wouldn't it pass through in another instant? Let time fly? But from now on this feeling couldn't exist for me. All beautiful women love to be pursued, and they are right. You all the more so. You haven't forgotten the one to whom you cried, "Yes, yes, yes," and my ordinary face couldn't possibly dim in your memory the face of that exotic, unbelievable man. I am dead as far as love is concerned.

Then she opened the door and came in—a short, quiet beauty with sloping shoulders. "I love you!" my whole being shouted. I understood that the childhood of my new life had passed and that I was now an adolescent.

And I heard a chilling noise at the window—and I didn't even have to turn to look. I knew.

Hardly having greeted the woman, I grabbed the notebook from her hand, turned my back on her, opened the book, and saw the rough draft and the calculations, the very same ones I had recklessly thrown away and burned. I leafed through the notebook. So! Not ten years, but eight! I'll work at the institute and at home. That makes two years. I'll set up the experiments so that they'll go in several directions at once. Day and night.

"Why are you hurrying?" the woman asked, seeing how quickly I was getting my equipment together and all set up.

"I have little time left," I said, and stopped short. "Life is short and I have much work. I'm in a hurry."

I set up all the apparatus and started a bright fire in the retorts. Limpid boiling streams began to run through the glass tubes, and rare essences began to form in the crucible.

My owl was sleeping under the window with its head under its wing. I decided to check one thing and rid myself of my last doubt.

"What is that under the window?" I asked the woman unexpectedly, and pointed to the owl.

At these words the huge bird raised its head and rapidly blinked its yellow eyes. The woman went to the window, leaned against the glass, and shielded her eyes from the light.

"There is no one there," she said, smiling. But suddenly she fell silent. She began to look at me intently, biting her lip, as if struck by some sort of new thought. "There is no one there," she repeated. "But have you seen anyone? Are they following you?"

"No, not that." I dodged answering.

And suddenly she asked me a question. Her turn had come to surprise me, to nonplus me. She asked, "Why did you change rooms?"

I was taken aback but stiffened and did not answer her. I was already living in the grip of a new discipline. I began to twirl the knob of my old arithmometer—I had to make some calculations. Not turning away, the woman stared at me.

After about an hour she couldn't restrain herself and began to laugh quietly.

"At least tell me where you are hurrying to."

"Where? One man—you know of whom I'm speaking—probably already told you where he was hurrying."

"He told . . ."

"Well, that's where I'm hurrying. I've lived an entire life and haven't yet done a thing. But I can give something to the people. I will have no rest on earth until someone squeezes my hand so that my heart jumps. I will work for him. He will come—and that will be a happy day."

She must have liked these words. She was silent for a while, but then again took herself in hand.

"Why are you wasting time? That's hardly like you. Why, you have a new, perfected calculating machine."

More surprises! What sort of new machine? Again I didn't answer her. Then she took me by the hand and led me toward the door.

"What now?" I stopped.

"Don't lose time," she said, mimicking me. "Don't be afraid! I can win time for you."

She dragged me into the other apartment, where a month ago my unusual comrade, the bandit, had lived. She took out a key, opened the door of his room, switched on the light, and turned away from me, hiding a smile. For I was really beaming. In the room stood the most expensive new equipment, precisely the sort I needed. I began to inspect it, to move it about, and quite forgot about my companion.

"Aren't you ashamed?" I suddenly heard her voice. "Pretending that you've never seen these things."

Again after her own goal.

"What do you mean by that?" I asked sharply.

"Well, you must have at least dropped in on your comrade," she answered evasively. "Is it possible that you didn't even see this?"

On the window sill, in a tank, there was growing a large white flower which had a strong scent but which was unfamiliar to me. The woman led me to it. She looked at me intently. And suddenly I remembered.

"This is a lotus. It was cultivated from the seed that lay in the tomb two thousand . . ."

"Ah ha!" she said in delight. "I grade you 'A plus.' And are you familiar with this?"

And she handed me a small calculator of the latest model—the sort of which I hadn't even dared to dream. This instrument could replace a whole department of men working with arithmometers.

"Can I take this?" I couldn't restrain myself.

"You are wasting time!" She raised her voice, now mimicking the bandit, now me. "Yes, yes, yes. This is all yours. All the equipment. Even the lotus!"

It occurred to me that she seemed insulted by something.

"Well, it's clear," she suddenly said thoughtfully. "You changed your face, your voice, and had to change rooms so that no one would know, no one say anything. . . . Even friends. . . ."

Earlier I would have mused over these words. But I've already said I was in the grip of a new discipline that set up everything in my head in a new way. I simply dismissed her chatter.

In a single night I had made a huge leap forward in my work. I became convinced that my old hypotheses were correct. If I went ahead on this track, I would get my first results in eight months, and then it would be

possible to throw the entire institute into the work. All the skeptics would lay down their arms.

Noticing nothing around me, full of the most joyous hopes, I went in the morning to our laboratory. While still at the door I heard some gay noise. It seems that my opponent S. had already squeezed out an answer to my article.

"What tactics!" exclaimed our boss, and after each of his words gaily threatening noises surged up.

They were all standing around my desk. The boss was chuckling, holding his belly; and there was missing from the famous picture only the scribe with his pen behind his ear—that is, myself.

"Well, dear warrior, now it's your turn," said the boss, laying the newspaper excerpt before me on the desk.

But I surprised them. I didn't even begin to read the article of this S., who now seemed to me simply a naïve and in no way dangerous crank. He no longer kindled my blood; another fire burned in it. I brushed him away like a mosquito. But I should say—getting ahead of the story—that this S. continued for a long time to print his articles especially for me. In one footnote he wrote that I had become silent from shame, in another that I had donned the blinkers of silence, that I was serving my time in the bush, that I had hidden my head like an ostrich. He crowed from afar and clapped his wings like a rooster, enticing me to continue the battle.

Watching me put the newspaper clipping aside, my comrades exchanged glances.

"What's the matter with you?" asked the practical joker in amazement. "Look, he hasn't shaved, it seems. Friends, he has thrown his coat on a chair. So that's how it is! His coat is missing two buttons. Don't you think he's changed? He's beginning to look like the one who used to sit beside him."

He looked pointedly at the bandit's empty chair.

And it was true; my character had changed greatly. I had become a different person. I suddenly forgot all my mannerisms of a great scientist. I stopped talking in a singsong voice, stopped running around cooing over stupid questions. I moved continuously in an intense, dreamlike state. A new desire for life awoke in me. And how strangely my ideas of pleasure had changed!

What were my pleasures? To look at her all the time. She set herself up beautifully in my room; brought over her bed and pillow, and worked at the experiments day and night. I don't even know when she slept. I enjoyed watching her from afar as she sat at the table. I fell in love with the thrust of her head and neck; she looked like a mother bending over her child.

And looking at the lines of her head and neck and sloping shoulders, at the sweet arc by which I always recognized her, I dreamed; I wanted her to turn around and look at me. She would always obey my silent order and turn around, resting her chin on her shoulder. But something would always bother her, and she would turn back to her work.

We had one rule: if we were waiting for a result in our work, we had to take a walk for an hour or two—to an exhibition, to the opera, or to a concert. One night, after leaving the apparatus and putting away the equipment, she took me by the hand.

"We have some free time. A whole hour. Can you give it to me?"

Very good, it's yours, I thought to myself.

We went out. She was taking me somewhere down a dark alley.

Suddenly she asked, "You really don't remember this street?"

I was bored with all this, and I didn't hide my annoyance. "All right, you've gotten on familiar terms with me. Fine. But I beg you to drop this strange game you've been playing for two months and which I don't understand. It's wasting our time."

"Where are you going in such a hurry?"

At that moment I saw in the shadow of the street lamp the dark shape of my owl and its brilliant blinking eyes. I stopped. I wanted to show those eyes to my companion, but I knew she wouldn't see anything.

"Where am I going?" I decided to tell her. "Here's where. I have less than a year to live."

My words affected her greatly. If I had said anything

more she would have burst into tears. She stopped me, stepped in front of me, and cupped my chin in her hands. I saw that her eyes were filled with tears.

"If you are so sure that it's less than a year, why are we deceiving each other?" she whispered.

I started to open my mouth to speak, but she put her fingers over my lips.

"You know it's you, you!"

"Do you think I'm *he?*"

"Don't torture me any more. Remember how you hid from me the first time. What are you punishing me for?"

"But I'm a different person!" I shouted. "Look, my hair and face are different! But *I* haven't changed. There are no skin-graft scars here. That's all me."

"You had no scars the first time. I guessed. I guessed right away. Tell me, when I first came to you with the note and the watch, didn't you suddenly ask yourself: 'Did she love him?' You wanted to know very much. I saw how naïve you were." She burst out laughing. "Do you know how happy that made me?"

"I'm going to leave you soon," I said.

"We'll never part. I'll find you even if you run away from me, get a new face, even change your height."

"I have less than a year to live. That's certain."

"I don't believe it. You'll be saying that for many years."

"You know who said that, and they killed him."

"They didn't kill him! You're clever; you thought it

all up. You made up this double. You're clever! They'll never get you!"

"Oh hell, this is stupid."

This cut her off. She laughed. "I won't talk about it. You never liked it. You're nicer than you used to be. You're softer; you smile! You talk well about the work you are doing. I've lost so much time. Why did I let myself play with you like a seventeen-year-old? Do you want me to give you the word you asked for? Yes! Yes! Do you hear? Shout to me that you hear!"

"I hear you," I whispered. I couldn't resist any more. The sliver went over the waterfall. "Whom do you love more?" I asked. "The one who is dead or the one who is next to you?"

"This one."

I was loved. I saw her eyes. I had only to move my head to the right and I saw two stars twinkling with tears.

And I took the place of the bandit. From adolescence I passed into maturity.

But the doctor had predicted correctly: five or six months after my meeting with him, I began to feel sick. One bright summer day I had to go to bed. I said guiltily to my love, who was watching silent and perplexed, "You know, dear one, it's hard for me to work. You'll have to take charge by yourself while I stay in bed. Turn on the radio."

She turned it on and suddenly the voice of our dark continent was heard, loudly sometimes and then drowned out in static. They were working there, digging coal and growing cabbages under artificial light.

"We'll have to be more energetic," I said. "We must hurry."

And the boiling bubbles in the glass tubes ran still faster and the fires burned more brightly.

We finished our work on one of the installations in rainy September. I lay in bed and was so weak that I couldn't raise my head.

"Open the first lead cowl," I said.

"An error," I heard her quiet voice. "Here there is only a small reddish piece of coal."

"No, that's not an error," I answered calmly. "That's only a variant. Everything is calculated for the other installations. But this piece of coal can already tell us to . . . Call the boss. Call the crew . . ."

They came in walking on tiptoe, as is proper when one goes to see a sick person. Earlier, I hadn't let them see me; and now, coming into my room which had been converted into a laboratory, they stopped at the door and stood and gazed round. They didn't know what to think. Everything surprised them: the walls covered with formulas and the furniture scratched up by a nail—I had written even on it—and the glitter of instruments from which little bubbles of heat went out to them.

Then they saw me. My appearance must have shocked

them; they became even quieter. Only the practical joker, who hadn't taken his eyes off my love, whispered something to the boss.

"Give them a report," I said.

And she, like a real scholar, gave them a ten-minute report on our work and showed them the piece of coal that still didn't want to cool off for anything.

This piece of coal surprised everyone, especially the boss. He first came ceremoniously to shake my hand. And all my comrades grew noisy and, vying with each other, threw themselves toward me and grasped my weak, light hands and began to squeeze them. And I felt my heart jump.

"Starting today, we will put the whole laboratory to work on this."

From that day two of our technicians began to keep watch day and night in my room, and every day they telephoned data to me from the laboratory. Things progressed quickly.

In cold December, in the presence of the boss, my love opened the second cowl.

"Again an error," she said quietly to the boss. "This time it's worse. The piece of coal is quite black."

But I heard them.

"That error was also calculated." I hardly moved my lips. "Continue to work. Faster!"

I had perfect hearing. I heard the boss, covering his mouth with his hand, whisper: "A third will kill him."

And he added loudly, "Hmm . . . I suggest that it would be better to carry the third installation to our laboratory. Then we can verify the experiment more quickly and precisely."

"I entrust it to you," I said.

And now my wife and I remained alone in the quiet, empty room. We two—and the owl, which one day contrived to squeeze through the glass vent to us, and now dozed on the window sill or roamed under the table, tapping with his beak along the floor. My wife—she really deserved that name—sat by me and we quietly recalled our brief youth.

On the third or fourth day I felt worse and asked, "Open the window."

"Sweetheart, it's freezing outside. Must I?"

"Open, open," I whispered.

My wife went to the window.

"What's this! Spring in December! On the street it is thawing and the flies have awakened and are buzzing against the glass."

"Open."

She opened just the glass vent at first and then the whole window. A warm spring breeze entered the room with an extraordinarily pleasant and distant music which played over the city, sometimes quietly and sometimes in a great wave. I listened and did not know that it was the sound of telephone wires informing the whole world of man's victory over cold and darkness. From time to

time a majestic sound that moved out into the distance
united with the sound of the music—this was the sound
of airplanes flying over the city with the first precious
load of light to the dark continent. But I did not know
this. I was in a bad way. I was so weak I didn't even
listen to hear if my friends were coming with good
news. And the owl frightened me again. It was going
around my bed in some strange state of excitement, flapping its wings. There is nothing worse than having to
leave life without completing something needed by man.

Then I dropped off to sleep. There was a noise on
the stairs, doors banged, hurried footsteps scraped on the
floor. But I didn't hear them. I heard only the voice of
the doctor, my school friend. "He's still alive!" he said.

He sat down at my bedside and began to unscrew a
little lead bulb with trembling hands.

Quickly! quickly! I wanted to shout.

And then I did shout, because my sickness had left
me.

A blinding flash quivered in the doctor's hands, filling
the whole room with sunlight. I had known this light
for a long time—in my dreams; with my eyes closed I had
seen it way back when I had first set up my equipment.
But in that moment I couldn't look at the midget sun's
bright light. I got up on shaking legs. My love ran to
help me, but I pushed her away and walked around the

room by myself. I even stamped my feet. She fell against the wall in disbelief.

"Thank you, Doctor," she whispered.

"For what? He conquered his own death. He found his own cure. It's his light!"

There was another sound on the staircase, the doors opened, and in burst a crowd of people, some of them comrades and some others I didn't know. They surrounded me. Someone shook my hand. My boss edged up to me. "So you managed to squeeze out some life after all!" he congratulated me. "In the old days they would have drawn an owl next to your name! You once suggested that the hieroglyph . . . remember?"

"You know, it was true," I said, and I thought, I really did squeeze my time out. I had lived a whole life in one year. And how many more years were before me—an entire ocean of time.

Whom should I thank for this? I looked out on the window sill where my owl always used to sit. It wasn't there. Only the lotus blossomed in the glass tank. But far, far out in the pale blue sky of spring some kind of huge bird was flying toward the horizon, heavily flapping its wings.

The ocean of time sparkled at my feet. I stood on the bank ready to begin my life again, and waves of the future washed over my feet, one after the other, urging me on. Tomorrow I'll be sailing on the far side of the

horizon. But I was a little afraid: for a year I had been used to the constant presence of the owl. Could I live without its reminders? Would this mighty ocean turn into a tiny stream which I would scarcely notice as I crossed it?

Then I remembered the watch and I grew cold with fear—my watch was making no sound.

I grabbed the watch chain. Of course! It had stopped! It had to be wound every year.

I got out the watch and inserted the key and turned it twenty times. There! Done! It was running. It was running in a New Year.

DUTTON EVERYMAN PAPERBACKS

DUTTON EVERYMAN PAPERBACKS